READERS SAY

"I REALLY LOVE TINKLE MASH-UPS!"
Nandika Suprabha
Bengaluru

"SUPERB! TINKLE ALWAYS COMES UP WITH SUPERCOOL IDEAS."
Jahnavi Grampurohit
New Delhi

"I WISH FOR MORE TOONS IN THE MASH-UPS!"
Rutuja Balraj
Thane, Maharashtra

"MY FAVOURITE IS THE MASH-UPS."
Sanjana
Visakhapatnam, Andhra Pradesh

"MASH-UPS ARE SUPERCOOL!"
Saanvi A.
Mysuru, Karnataka

INTR

It's time for yet another rollercoaster ride with the *Tinkle* Toons!

Tinkle mash-up stories have always been at the top of the most-requested list from readers. There's something about seeing Suppandi, Tantri the Mantri, Shikari Shambu and other Tinkle Toons in the same story. Now it's time for yet another instalment of these Toons ganging up! And this time round, there are three exclusive, never-before-seen stories of the Toons embarking on the most bizarre adventures of their lifetime!

So take a trip to a haunted summer camp, dive deep under the ocean, tour the kingdom of Hujli, be a hero on a strange island, and plod through the mysterious world of Greek gods. All this and more, when you join Suppandi and friends!

Plus! Suppandi answers readers' questions!

Plus! More exclusive goodies in the form of art and script snapshots in a special Behind the Scenes feature!

Hair in the Scare	3
The Tinkle Talk Show with Kooki	18
Sense and Nonsense	19
Suppandi: Bon Appétit	20
Shikari Shambu: Wild Shots	21
Dark Zone	22
Suppandi: The Interview	30
Jumble Dumble	31
Kooki Scoops	32
Ina Mina Mynah Mo & Tantri The Mantri : Vacation Action	34
Little Suppandi: The Test	42
Thought Reader	46
Just for Fun	47
Suppandi: Swimming Pool Rules	48
Island Insanity	49
Ask Suppandi	64
Shambu's Wild Shots	65
Suppandi: Choked!	66
The Tinkle Talk Show with Kooki	67
Brain Teasers	68
Suppandi Was Here!	69
Hide 'N' Greek	70
Behind the Scenes	85

*Suppandi is a loveable goof who takes everything literally

The TINKLE TALK Show
with Kooki

Hi! My name is Kooki, and I am the bigggggessssst fan of the *Tinkle* toons. That's why I chase them, catch them and ask them all the questions that I've always wanted to ask them. Woof! Look who I caught, er... interviewed this time!

Ravi from Defective Detectives*

What advice would you give to aspiring detectives?
– Abhinav Pandey, via email

Get a new aspiration. Don't get me wrong. I'm not being rude. It's just real real talk. And I say this for two reasons.
One, being a detective means a lot of hard work. It's not as easy as we make it look. And not everybody's cut out for this job. Like, you need serious above-average intelligence, presence of mind and imagination, like ours.
Two, even if you do become a detective, you will have no case to solve... because we would have solved it before you! Ha-ha-ha!
Right, Rahul? *hi-fives*

Tantri the Mantri**

What is the first thing you plan to do on becoming King of Hujli?
– Abhay V. P, via email

When I'll become king, no one will be able to stop me from doing many 'first things', will they now? So, the moment I wear the crown (and finish admiring myself in the mirror, of course), I will start removing all traces of that toxic Hooja from my kingdom, starting with its name. 'Hujli' shall be changed to 'Tantrinagar'. Then, all statues of Hooja will be reshaped to look like me, all coins shall be stamped with my face, all books shall be rewritten to glorify me. I will make everything remind the people of me, their great king. In fact, I think I'll order everyone to tattoo my name on their arms. Let's see another king beat that! Muhaha!

Kalia the Crow#

Who looks after Big Baan when you're away?

You know the old saying 'when the cat is away, the mouse is at play'? Well, that's truer with Chamataka and Doob Doob than anyone else. So, I've actually devised several plans to make sure that the animals are taken care of when I'm away from Big Baan. I always provide Bholu with honey and, in return, he keeps an eye out for me. I also ask several of my cousins to fly high above Chamataka and Doob Doob when they are stalking prey. After all these years, even my shadow seems to send shivers down their spines.

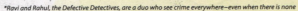

*Ravi and Rahul, the Defective Detectives, are a duo who see crime everywhere–even when there is none
**Tantri the Mantri will do anything to get rid of Raja Hooja and become king of Hujli instead
#Kalia is the avaian protector of Big Baan forest

SENSE AND NONSENSE

ART: ABHIJEET KINI | COLOURIST: ADARSH ACHARI

In Eltham Park South, London, there's a crow who seems to have a grouse against female blondes. It lies in wait in the trees and the moment it sees a female blond jogger, dive-bombs to attack. It has attacked five joggers so far, badly scratching their hands and faces.
A crow expert says it might have had a bad experience with a blonde.

A restaurant called 'Wafu' near Sydney, Australia, is enforcing a new policy of charging customers 30 per cent more if they don't finish all the food they've ordered. The restaurant, specializing in Japanese food, expects diners to eat everything on their plate, including the garnishing and the salad or other food accompanying the main dish. If a customer wastes too much or is a habitual waster, he or she is advised not to come again. There is a mixed response from customers, but the restaurant continues to do good business.

At the World Snail Racing Championship, an event that has been held every year for the last 40 years, Sidney, the snail, raced to victory, covering the distance of 13 inches in the astonishing time of 3 minutes and 41 seconds! The snail's owner, Claire Lawrence was thrilled but Sidney himself showed no emotion as he was presented with his prize – a silver cup stuffed with lettuce!

*Mapui, a seemingly ordinary girl, turns into WingStar, a crime-fighting superhero

SUPPANDI THE INTERVIEW

Story & Script
Shruti Dave

Pencils & Inks
Archana Amberkar

Colours
Umesh Sarode

Letters
Prasad Sawant

KOOKI SCOOPS

As the biggggggest *Tinkle* fan ever, I always wonder what my favourite toons do when the magazine is closed. Just like me, I'm sure you've heard their stories. You've seen them fly, stumble, fall, pack a punch, and in some cases get punched! But what do our dear *Tinkle* toons say and think about each other? Read on; you might just be surprised by what you find out!

A friendly note from unfriendly Tantri: *Be careful of what you believe, readers! Just like my plans, Kooki's sources are often defective. But don't forget, there's no smoke without fire. And I must now go and light a not-so-friendly fire for my dear king Hooja! Muahahaha!*

WingStar's Cheesy Secret

With her powerful jetpacks, WingStar manages to remain out of reach. But according to unreliable sources, WingStar, who complains about not having any free time, was recently spotted petting a dog! Does that mean WingStar spends her free time eating cheese popcorn and watching puppy videos on the Internet? Does that mean WingStar secretly wants a pet dog? Will she name it Bow WOW? Are we going to see WingDog take over the skies with WingStar? Surely, a super dog would be a perfect sidekick for a superhero!

Mynah: The Puppet Master

Psst! A new rumour has been flying around *Tinkle* Town. Aspiring author, Mynah, from Ina Mina Mynah Mo, secretly controls all *Tinkle* writers! The writers deny this but who believes writers anyway?! To confirm these strange whispers, I followed Mynah for two days and two nights. I overheard her saying, "I'm sending those writers some writing tips." Does that mean the *Tinkle* writers are Mynah's puppets? Taking advice and orders from her? If so, then the *Tinkle* Toons seem to be in good hands.

Sam Speaks

Kooki(K): Sam! What's your favourite colour?
Sam(S): Blue. It shows strength, honesty and reliability—all the qualities a detective should possess.

K: Who do you consider your biggest competition?
S: *Smirking* I will have to say 'myself'! The Defective Detectives like to call themselves my competition. Thankfully, everyone knows that they are nothing but a couple of bumbling baboons.

K: What is your biggest secret?
S: I have no secrets, but I'll tell you one about Rahul and Ravi. The two geniuses believe that sleeping with a detective book under the pillow can make them better detectives. If only they read the book instead of sleeping on it there would be some hope for them! Hahaha!

BEHIND THE SCENES

Did you know that Leher got her SuperWeird power from *Tinkle* Editor-in-Chief Rajani Thindiath's eternal struggle with her own hair?! Rajani's hair has a life of its own. If unleashed on the world, it can wreak havoc. So she needs to tie her hair up well and good so it doesn't escape. Rajani's tussle with her curls translated into Leher's SuperWeird locks!

QUICK FACTS WITH KOOKIE

Our friendly conservationist Shikari Shambu is a great cook but is just too lazy to actually cook!

As a child Shambu spent all his free time hanging around the kitchen of his favourite restaurant, Hotel Khao. The restaurant's chef, Khao Sway, and Shambu soon became great friends. Mr. Sway taught Shambu all his top secret culinary arts. Rumour has it that Shambu makes the best *medu vadas* in the whole of *Tinkle* Town! Sigh! Do you think I'll ever be invited to lunch by Shikari Shambu some day?

Ravi vs Rahul: Who's the Boss?

AS BEST FRIENDS GO, RAVI AND RAHUL RANK NUMBER ONE IN THE WORLD! BUT MANY READERS (INCLUDING ME) WONDER WHO THE BOSS IS IN TEAM DEFECTIVE DETECTIVES. I CALLED BOTH RAVI AND RAHUL AND HERE'S WHAT THEY HAD TO SAY!

Kooki? Do you promise this phone is not being tapped by spies? Aliens? Sam?!

But I trust you. So I will tell you that I think **I** am the true leader of our team. A leader has to… erm… lead! Act! And I do that.

But don't tell Rahul that! He's my best friend.

Are you really Kooki? Or are you a clone talking in Kooki's voice?!

Even if you are, let me tell you, **I** am the brains behind all our missions. Which makes me the leader. Clearly. *Duh*

But don't you dare tell Ravi that! There can be no arguments between Agent Big Brain and Agent Bulging Brawn.

THESE TWO DETECTIVES COULD BE DEFECTIVE BUT THEIR FRIENDSHIP DEFINITELY ISN'T!

Text: Ritu Mahimkar   Layout: Prasad Sawant

Little Suppandi — THE TEST

Story Elias Hussain **Script** Sean D'mello **Pencils & Inks** Archana Amberkar **Colourist** Umesh Sarode **Letters** Pranay Bendre

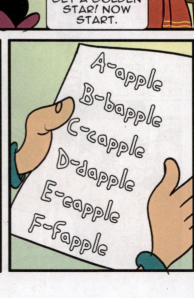

ARE YOU GETTING YOUR REQUIRED TINKLE DOSAGE EVERY MONTH?

Get 100+ pages of brand new Tinkle adventures at your doorstep!

FREE Fun with Suppandi pack of 4

TINKLE MAGAZINE

☐ 1 Year (24 issues) + Fun with Suppandi pack of 4
MRP ₹960/-

☐ 1 Year (24 issues)
Offer Price ₹849/-

FREE Tinkle Celebration Pack 1

TINKLE COMBO
TINKLE MAGAZINE + TINKLE DIGEST

☐ 1 Year (36 issues) + Tinkle Celebration Pack 1
MRP ₹1800/-

☐ 1 Year (36 issues)
Offer Price ₹1649/-

YOUR DETAILS*

Name: .... Date of birth: ☐☐☐☐☐☐☐☐

Address: ....

City: .... State: .... Pin Code: ☐☐☐☐☐☐

School: .... Email: ....

Phone/Mobile No.: ☐☐☐☐☐☐☐☐☐☐

PAYMENT OPTIONS

Cheque/DD: ☐☐☐☐☐☐ drawn in favour of 'ACK MEDIA DIRECT LTD.' on bank ....
.... for amount ....
.... Dated ☐☐☐☐☐☐☐☐ and send it to:
AFL House, 7th Floor, Lok Bharti Complex, Marol Maroshi Road, Andheri East, Mumbai- 400059.

☐ PAY AN ADDITIONAL ₹300 TO RECEIVE COPIES BY COURIER

Please allow four to six weeks for your subscription to begin!

THOUGHT READER

HEY! NOW YOU CAN GUESS WHAT'S ON YOUR FRIEND'S MIND! JUST USE THE 'THOUGHT READER' CHART AND FOLLOW THE INSTRUCTIONS GIVEN BELOW.

551	234	324	492	481	317	227	306
369	52	142	310	299	135	45	124
324	7	97	265	254	90	0	79
462	145	235	403	392	228	138	217
328	11	101	269	258	94	4	83
667	350	440	608	597	433	343	422
326	9	99	267	256	92	2	81
460	143	233	401	390	226	136	215

1. Show the chart to your friend and ask him/her to circle any number on the chart.
2. Next ask him/her to cross out all the numbers in that row (left and right of the selected number) and that column (top and bottom of the selected number).
3. Ask him/her to repeat steps 1 & 2 in the other columns, till he/she has selected eight numbers and crossed off the remaining numbers.
4. Now tell him/her to add the eight numbers.
5. When your friend finishes adding, proudly announce that the sum of the numbers selected by him/her is 2011!
6. Your friend will be amazed by your psychic skills!

Secret of the Trick:
The numbers in the 'Thought Reader' chart have been arranged in such a manner that sum of any eight numbers will always be 2011! (Please be sure that your friend chooses the numbers as per the instructions or he/she may have a different answer!)

IDEA: SUMITA BOSE

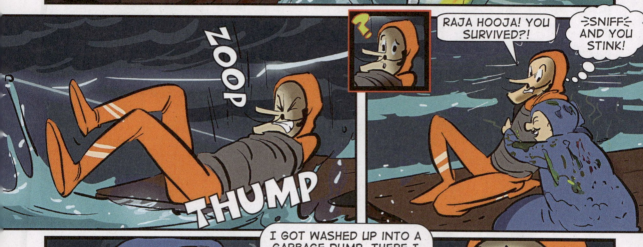

TERRIFIC TINKLE COLLECTIONS
JUST A CLICK AWAY!

Best of Tinkle Assorted Digests
(Pack of 20)
₹1400

Tinkle Assorted Digests
(Pack of 24)
₹1649

Tinkle Assorted Digests
(Pack of 50)
₹3459

Best of Tinkle Assorted Double Digests
(Pack of 5)
₹600

Best of Tinkle Assorted Double Digests
(Pack of 10)
₹1199

Tinkle Assorted Double Digests
(Pack of 24)
₹2669

Fabulous 50 Tinkle Double Digests-Vol 2
(Pack of 50)
₹5849

Tinkle Celebrations Pack 1
₹699

Tinkle Celebrations Pack 2
₹899

Tinkle Celebrations Pack 3
₹1199

Tantri the Mantri-The Essential Collection
(Pack of 7)
₹875

Adventures with Shambu
(Pack of 7)
₹875

Tinkle Special Collection-Vol 1
(Pack of 3)
₹349

Tinkle Special Collection-Vol 2
(Pack of 3)
₹349

Tinkle Special Collection-Vol 3
(Pack of 3)
₹349

Tinkle Special Collection-Vol 4
(Pack of 3)
₹349

Tinkle Special Collection-Vol 5
(Pack of 3)
₹349

Tinkle Special Collection-Vol 6
(Pack of 3)
₹349

Superstars of Tinkle
(Pack of 17)
₹1999

Folktales from Around The World
(Pack of 4)
₹450

Tinkle Folktales from Around The World
(Pack of 9)
₹999

Suppandi-The Essential Collection
(Pack of 9)
₹1199

LOG ON TO WWW.AMARCHITRAKATHA.COM
OR CALL US AT 022 4918 888 1/2 TO PLACE YOUR ORDER TODAY!

Ask Suppandi

Have you always had a burning question that no one could answer? Well, don't fear because I, Suppandi, am here! I give you my guarantee—just like my boss' instructions, I'll listen to all your questions carefully and answer them a hundred percent honestly. So ask away!

Vedant Chowdhury asks, "What came first, the chicken or the egg?"

Come on, Vedant, be reasonable. How could either of them have come first when neither of them had run a race? Or participated in any competitions? To answer this question, you need to make the chicken and the egg do something. Challenge them to draw a picture of a house, perhaps. Or bake a cake. And make sure you have a whistle. When you blow the whistle, both the chicken and the egg should start whatever task you have set for them. Whoever completes the task first comes first! Simple!

Avanti Bane from Mumbai asks, "How can we teach ourselves good manners?"

Excellent question, Avanti! Everyone needs to have good manners, even villains like Tantri. So here's how you can teach yourself good manners. First, bring out your blackboard or whiteboard and position it in front of a mirror. Then, grab some chalk or a marker. Now start talking about good manners like a teacher would in a classroom. For example, say something like, "Say 'please' and 'thank you' to people," and then write it down on the board. And since you're standing in front of a mirror, everything you say, your reflection will say back to you. And hey presto! You would have then taught yourself good manners!

Ishwar Prasanna Hazarika from Guwahati, Assam asks, "Will volcanoes erupt again?"

Ishwar, the honest answer to that question is—yes. Yes, volcanoes will erupt again, if they want to. You see, nobody can make anybody do anything they don't want to. I'll give you an example. My best friend Maddy was invited to his school reunion party. He wanted to look his best at the party. But a day before the event, a big, fat, red boil erupted on his nose! Now, Maddy didn't want the boil, but the boil wanted to be there (and probably attend the party too). Maddy tried lots of face creams and ointments, but the erupted boil didn't go anywhere. So he gave up and went to the party with it. The boil must have really enjoyed itself because the very next day after the party, it went away.

SHAMBU'S WILD SHOTS

COME, LET ME GIVE YOU A PERSONALIZED TOUR OF THE BEAUTY IN THE WILDERNESS!

Photo Courtesy and Text: Mr. Shyam Ghate,
Wildlife Enthusiast and Photographer
Illustrations & layout: Savio Mascarenhas

FIRST STOP: ANDAMAN ISLANDS. TO MEET OUR FRIEND, THE ANDAMAN DAY GECKO*.

Isn't she beautiful? The Andaman Day Gecko (Latin name: *Phelsuma andamanense*) is found only in the Andaman Islands in the Bay of Bengal. Its green, slender body has red stripes and dots. What you are seeing me shoot here is a female Andaman Day Gecko. The males have a turquoise blue tail.

*Gecko is a kind of lizard that is usually found in warm climates around the world. All geckos are lizards, but all lizards are not geckos.

NOW YOU MIGHT ASK—HOW ARE THESE GECKOS DIFFERENT FROM THE ONES WE SEE AROUND OUR HOMES?

While the geckos you see on your house walls are active at night (nocturnal), the Phelsuma is active mainly during day time (diurnal) and is hence called Day Gecko. Like other Day Geckos, it has rounded pupils without eyelids; instead the pupils are covered with a clear, fixed sheet (plate) which the gecko regularly cleans with its tongue (icky though that sounds).

BUT WHY ARE THESE GECKOS FOUND ONLY IN THE ANDAMANS?

Actually, all coloured Geckos are supposed to have originated in the Madagascar Islands in the Indian Ocean which lie about 5,000 km away from the Andaman Islands. Perhaps this species must have accidentally got transported as part of cargo on a boat hundreds of years ago, and then made the Andamans their home. There, they must have evolved to adapt to the local environment. So today, you don't find anything like them anywhere else in the world. It is also possible that some human beings may have carried them as pets and then the animals spread and thrived in the wild. Scientific theories stop here.

SUPPANDI Choked!

Story & Script Pratik Dhruve   **Pencils & Inks** Archana Amberkar   **Colours** Umesh Sarode   **Letters** Prasad Sawant

The TINKLE TALK Show
with Kooki

Hi! My name is Kooki, and I am the biggggessssst fan of the *Tinkle* toons. That's why I chase them, catch them and ask them all the questions that I've always wanted to ask them. Woof! Look who I caught, er... interviewed this time!

Shikari Shambu

Woah, Shambu! You have a lot of fans! Abhay Sapnesh, Jyotisman Hazarika, Mythili Iyer, Tejaswi Giridhar, Monisha Rani, and Kaushika Murthy wrote in to me. They all want to know why you cover your eyes with a hat. Actually, I want to know that too. Hehe.

Well, Kooki, the truth is that, in my profession, there are a lot of dangers. And one must have a strategy to cope with them to survive. Otherwise, the wild will gobble you up like I gobble up Shanti's famous aloo parathas. Yummmm... Anyway, my strategy is my trusty hat. How, you ask? It's really simple. My hat helps me to face danger without having to look it in the eye. And if I don't look at danger directly, nothing can scare me! Nothing! That's how I have garnered the reputation of being brave and fearless. Which is what my fans love me best for, right?

Besides, I think that the hat suits me a lot, don't you? It's the perfect fashion statement for a famous personality like me (grins and twirls moustache).

Rahul from Defective Detectives

Gayathri P. wants to know what the steps to solving a case are. Oh, please tell us your secrets!

Ah, the subtle science of investigation, and deduction, and detection and... uh, other detective-y stuff. It's quite an art this science, you know. Because there are signs everywhere... you just need to have the eye to spot it! For example, to a layperson, a person throwing out trash might look like ordinary BUT, as a detective, you should never be sure of anything! TRUST NO ONE! For that person could be sending an illegal package in that trash bag through a secret tunnel under the trash bin. You must live by the rule—guilty until proven innocent if you want to get anywhere close to solving a mystery. Put yourself in the criminal's shoes, think like a criminal—and you'll see the hidden clues that'll lead you straight to the guilty. But, of course, you should leave stuff like this to the experts—us! ☺

Jagannath from Ina Mina Mynah Mo

Sana Fathima wanted to know if your daughters Ina, Mina, Mynah and Mo have the habit of saving money i.e. using a piggy bank?

These girls, I tell you! I'm always after them to save, save and save. But they never listen. However, they do save my money, in their own unique way. Ina and Mynah keep their eyes peeled for discounts so that they can get their clothes and books a little bit cheaper. Mina loves what Ina wears, so she doesn't mind the hand-me-downs. As for my darling, Mo, she loves to cook with Bina and that means fewer meals eaten out for the family. I wish they were more like their father, but, for now, as long as they save my money, I'm content.

67

SUPPANDI WAS HERE!

ART: ABHIJEET KINI

I TOLD HIM TO GIVE THE DOGS SOMETHING TO CHEW... AND HE GAVE THEM BUBBLE GUM!

I TOLD HIM TO "POLISH IT SPARKLING CLEAN!" AND HE USED SHOE POLISH!

HIDE 'N' GREEK

Story & Script Dolly Pahlajani **Art** Abhijeet Kini Studios **Letters** Satyawan Rane

*Billy Drain is a cowardly vampie without fangs

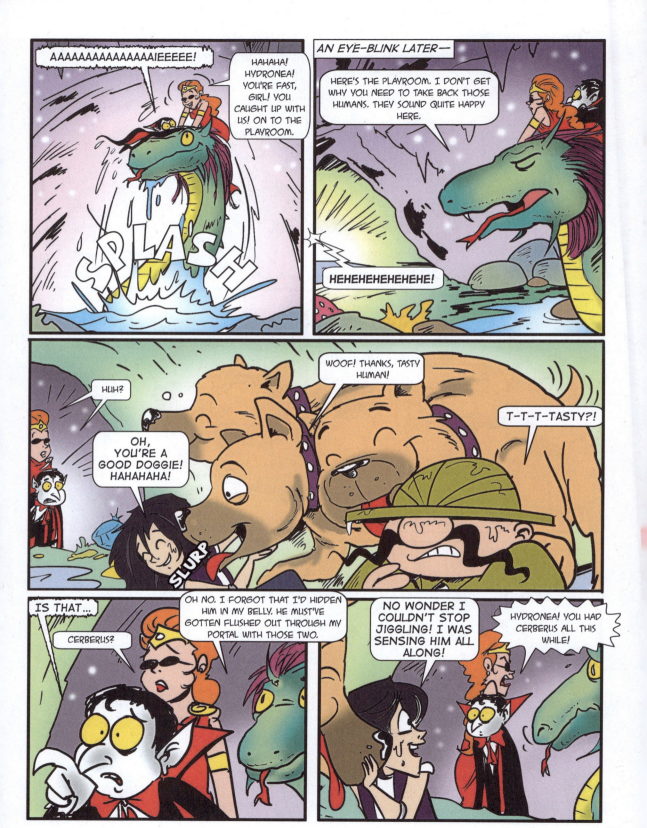

BEHIND THE SCENES

SUPPANDI AND FRIENDS 2

Hello folks! Suppandi and his friends really enjoyed getting together and going on adventures for this book. If you're wondering how these adventures came about, read on.

First, an idea came knocking at the writer's head. The writer spun it into a story. The story took the shape of a comics script before flying to the artist. Under the artist's hand, the characters of the story came alive, first as rough pencils, then in inks and colours. Then came the letterer to insert speech bubbles and give the characters speech. A check and recheck for errors by the editors and voila! The comic story is ready!

But between the idea and the ready comic there were tweaks and changes to the story and art. Turn the pages to check out what happened behind the scenes!

HIDE 'N' GREEK

BEHIND THE SCENES

4. Hey, Charon. You know what to do. (guard, calling out to the boatman as they exit the door right on to the banks of the river)
Yes, I do. Hop on, laddies and lassies. We need to make good time, tally ho! (Charon, cheerfully; Charon is a skeletal kind of figure and has taken to wearing one eye-mask with his toga)
Vis: The boat is a light canoe since it's actually meant for ferrying the dead. Not too much weight-carrying capacity here.

In writer Dolly Pahlajani's script, the fourth panel on the fourth page of the story is just a single panel, as seen above. But artist Abhijeet Kini wanted to split the dialogues here so that Hades' bodyguard first called out to Charon and then gave him instructions in the proceeding panel.

The very first draft of Dolly's script had many jokes that unfortunately couldn't make it to the final story. Here's one of the jokes that were cut. This was originally panel 2 on the third page of the story. Hades responds to Shambu after Shambu tells Hades that he's never heard of him.

2. But... er... surely you must've heard of me. Maybe studied about me in school? (Hades, deflating and prodding Shambu hopefully)
Erm... sorry. I didn't pay much attention to any subject besides biology. They were all Greek to me. (Shambu, embarrassed)

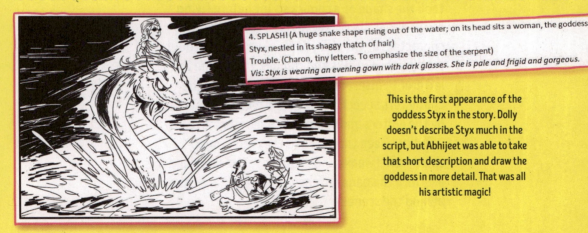

4. SPLASH! (A huge snake shape rising out of the water; on its head sits a woman, the goddess Styx, nestled in its shaggy thatch of hair)
Trouble. (Charon, tiny letters. To emphasize the size of the serpent)
Vis: Styx is wearing an evening gown with dark glasses. She is pale and frigid and gorgeous.

This is the first appearance of the goddess Styx in the story. Dolly doesn't describe Styx much in the script, but Abhijeet was able to take that short description and draw the goddess in more detail. That was all his artistic magic!

5. Cerberus was last seen near the river Styx. Charon, my ferryman, can help you search for him. (Hades)
Persephone dear, take them to Charon, would you? (Hades, talking without turning to the guard near him)
Yes, Lord. (Persephone, the female guard, nodding her head)

The first draft of the script also featured Persephone, Hades' wife, in a very minor role. This was originally panel 5 on the third page of the story. Persephone carried out tasks that Hades' bodyguard ended up doing in the final version.

BEHIND THE SCENES

HAIR IN THE SCARE

What's the circle on Suppandi's face? Was he wearing a monocle in an early draft of the story? No, that's just a skeletal framework artist Sahil Upalekar drew before fleshing out Suppandi. Sahil drew that circle as a guide, to ensure that he wouldn't make Suppandi's face wider than that circle while drawing over it. When he began inking the pages, he simply erased that circle since it had served its purpose.

Nobody can beat Suppandi when it comes to taking things literally. But how much of everyday speech does he misunderstand? Writer Aparna Sundaresan decided to test that with this Suppandi joke in her script that was originally supposed to run from page 2 to 3 of the story. Sadly, it didn't turn out to be as funny as she thought it was and she had to replace it with a joke about bedspreads in the final version!

2.4	Mo raises her hand enthusiastically.	Mo, raising hand, almost jumping up and down in excitement: Oh! Oh! Mr. Suppandi! What are you serving for dinner? Suppandi, taken aback: I'm not serving anything for dinner.
2.5	Suppandi points to a larger cottage some distance away. This is the kitchen-cum-dining area.	Mynah, confused: But you just said we should come back out for dinner. Suppandi, helpfully pointing to the kitchen cottage: Yes, because dinner is in that cottage there.
3.1	Suppandi walks away nonchalantly. In the background, Mynah and Mo look bewildered, while Buchki and Cyrus look at each other confused.	Suppandi, walking away nonchalantly: I didn't say I'd serve dinner. You must **listen** to instructions in this camp. Or you'll have a tough time. Now, hurry!

The final script only described Suppandi as sliding off the chair in these two panels. But Sahil made it 10 times funnier by having Suppandi scoot from the chair as fast as he could instead. And it's just as funny even as a rough pencil sketch!

In the very first draft of the script, only Buchki could see the Preta ghost right up to the very end. Well, if Suppandi, Mynah and Mo couldn't see the end of the Preta ghost, what fun would that be? So the script was changed for the final version so that sunlight made the ghost visible.

14.3	Mynah, Mo and Buchki open the windows and sunlight comes flooding into the room. The ghost looks in horror at the wig which is now ruined.	Mo, smug: Well, it's his own **prized** wig, Mr. Suppandi, so it's bound to be delicious… Ghost, screaming in disgust at the wig it has ruined: AAAHH! MY BEAUTIFUL WIIIG! WHAT HAVE I DOOOONE?!
14.4	The ghost dissolves into ash as Buchki looks on.	Ghost, dissolving into ash: NOOOOOO! Buchki, satisfied: Disgusted at ruining your stolen wig? Well, serves you right!

87

ISLAND INSANITY

BEHIND THE SCENES

This fabulous detective pose of the Defective Detectives showed up in panel 5 on the fourth page of the story in artist Sahil Upalekar's pencil roughs. But this had to be cut, alas, from the final story.

> **Collage:**
>
> **Vis 1:**
> Tantri is eating when Hooja is nudging him, knocking Tantri's spoon off.
>
> **Vis 2:**
> Tantri is sleeping when Hooja is poking his head in the door, scaring Tantri.
>
> **Vis 3:**
> Tantri is standing on the helm of the ship and Hooja is right behind him.
>
> **Vis 1:**
> **Hooja (excited):** Hey, are we there yet?!
> **Tantri (annoyed):** We set sail an *hour* ago, sire.
>
> **Vis 2:**
> **Caption:** Day two—
> **Hooja (excited):** Are we there yet?
> **Tantri (scared):** Aaah!
>
> **Vis 3:**
> **Caption:** Day seven—
> **Hooja (excited):** Are we there yet?
> **Tantri (excited):** Finally, we are!

In the first draft of the script for 'Island Insanity', a part of the story showed Tantri and Hooja's journey to Kooni Island. As if Tantri needed more reasons to be annoyed with Hooja!

Mapui looks pretty stylish in the story, doesn't she? But in the rough art, she was dressed plainly. Sahil gave her a couple of cool accessories later as he inked and coloured the pages.

Remember when Hooja almost drowned? What a thrilling moment, right? Well, in the script, this is how that moment was written by writer Ritu Mahimkar. Sahil took just a few lines of text and turned into a memorable scene!

> **7.1 Collage:**
>
> **Vis 1:**
> Hooja looks thrilled to be in the water.
>
> **Vis 2:**
> Hooja looks a little scared. The tides have started to pull him in the water.
>
> **Vis 3:**
> We see Hooja drowning inside the water.
>
> **Vis 1:**
> **SFX (water):** Splash
> **Hooja (thrilled):** This is fun. I see why Kooni kings do this—
>
> **Vis 2:**
> **Hooja (scared):** Aah! I'm getting dragged in!
>
> **Vis 3:**
> **Hooja (drowning):** HELP! TANTRI! HELP— {Blub} {Blub} {Blub}